To my uncle, Chris Marshall,
who plays in the snow in Alaska.

—K.W.

For Peter, Mary, Sarah, and Phil,
who live in a snowy place.

—With love, L.R.

Text copyright © 2005 by Karma Wilson
Illustrations copyright © 2005 by Laura Rader

Little, Brown and Company

Time Warner Book Group
1271 Avenue of the Americas, New York, NY 10020
Visit our Web site at www.lb-kids.com

First Edition: October 2005

Library of Congress Cataloging-in-Publication Data

Wilson, Karma.
  Dinos in the snow! / by Karma Wilson ; illustrated by Laura Rader.— 1st ed.
      p. cm.
  Summary: Dinosaurs enjoy many snow activities, from building snowmen and
snowball fights to skiing and skating.
  ISBN 0-316-00948-2
  [1. Snow—Fiction. 2. Dinosaurs—Fiction. 3. Stories in rhyme.] I. Rader,
Laura, ill. II. Title.
PZ8.3.W6976Dg 2005
[E]—dc22
                                                                    2004009894

10 9 8 7 6 5 4 3 2 1

Book design by Saho Fujii

TWP

Printed in Singapore

The illustrations for this book were done in Acrylics and ink on Strathmore bristol p
The text was set in Newboyd, and the display type was hand-lettered by Laura Rad

ALSO BY KARMA WILSON:

Dinos on the Go!
Never, Ever Shout in a Zoo
Mr. Murry and Thumbkin
Sakes Alive! A Cattle Drive

ALSO ILLUSTRATED BY LAURA RADER:

Dinos on the Go!

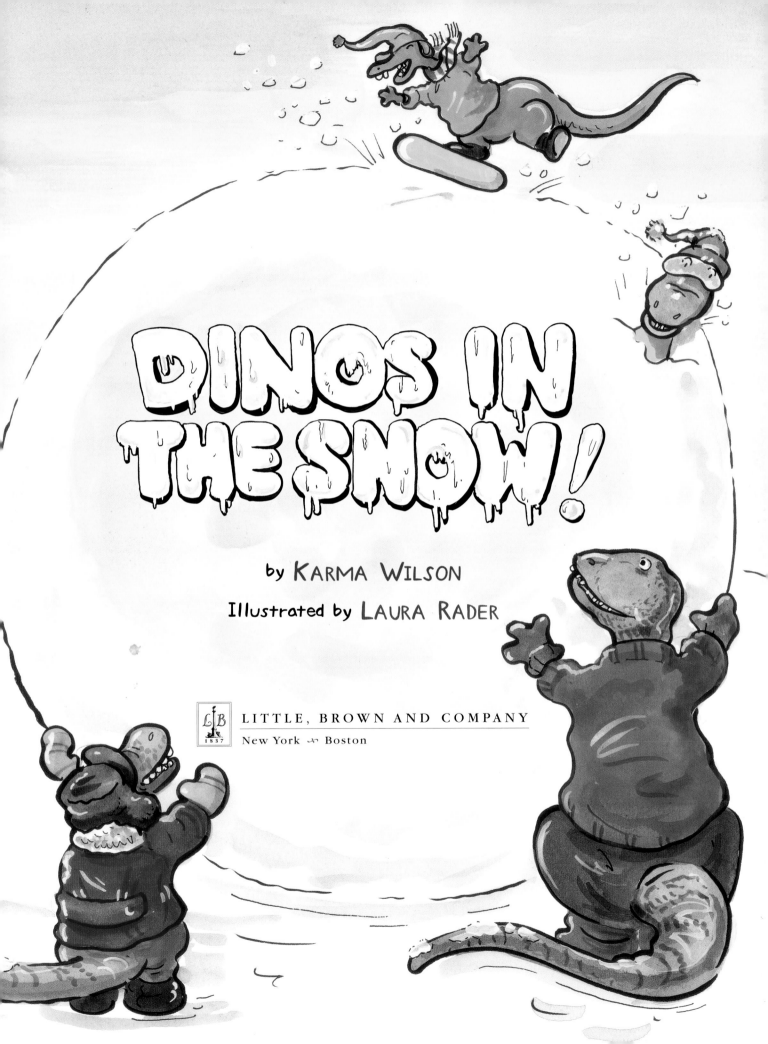

DINOS IN THE SNOW!

by KARMA WILSON

Illustrated by LAURA RADER

LITTLE, BROWN AND COMPANY
New York ⁓ Boston

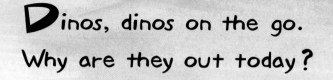

Dinos, dinos on the go.
Why are they out today?

To run and romp,
to slip and stomp
and ride their dino—sleigh.

Dinos, dinos in the snow.
But won't they catch the flu?
They're wearing boots
with fluffy suits,
hats, and mittens too.

Barapasaurus builds the biggest
snowman in the town.
It's leaning slightly to the side.
Oh no! It's falling down!

Dinos in the snow.
There they go!
BOOM BOOM!

Stegosaurus skates superbly.
Watch her glide with grace.
The crowd lets out a mighty cheer.
She's sure to win first place!

Dinos in the snow.
There they go!
WOO HOO!

Dilophosaurus dodges
to the left and to the right.
He moves so quick he's never lost
a single snowball fight.

Dinos in the snow.

There they go!

SPLIT SPLAT!

Dinos, dinos in the snow.
Where are they off to now?

What rotten luck.
They all got stuck.
They need a dino plow!

Dinos, dinos in the snow.
Hurray! They all got free.
They cheer and then
start out again.
They're headed off to ski!

STUCK IN THE SNOW?
CALL
TRICERA-PLOW
— and GO!!

Those dinos hit the snowy slopes.
Now watch those dinos go.
Geranosaurus slalom-jumps
and yells, "Geranimo!"

Dinos in the snow.
There they go!
WHISH WHOOSH!

Supersauras snowboards swiftly!
Wow, she sure can slide.
Look out! She's caused an avalanche
right down the mountainside.

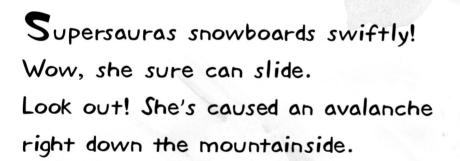

Dinos in the snow.
There they go!
SWISH SWOOSH!

T-rex tries tobogganing.
He's faster than the wind.
Let's hope he doesn't crash and burn
while headed round the bend.

Dinos in the snow.
There they go!
OH NO!

Dinos, dinos in the snow.
It's time to go warm up.

The fire roars.
Aunt Milly pours
hot cocoa in their cups.

CRETACEOUS CREME DONUTS

Dinos, dinos in the snow.
They're tuckered out tonight.
Now they're done
But, oh, what fun.
Today was dino-mite!